(sale)

Propeller One-Way
Night Coach

A FABLE FOR ALL AGES
John Travolta

WARNER BOOKS

A Time Warner Company

Presented by the Book Division of J.T.P. Films, Inc.

Warner Books, Inc., 1271 Avenue of the Americas, New York, NY 10020
Visit our Web site at http://warnerbooks.com

 A Time Warner Company

Printed in the United States of America

First Printing: October 1997

10   9   8   7   6   5   4   3   2   1

Library of Congress Cataloging-in-Publication Data
Travolta, John
     Propeller one-way night coach : a fable for all ages / by John Travolta.
        p.   cm.
     ISBN 0-446-52257-0
     I. Title.
   PS3570.R3533P76   1997
   813'.54—dc21   97-22596
                                                            CIP

Illustrations by John Travolta and Anson Downes

Adapted from the original design by McCoy Co.
Sam McCoy, Amy Ray Fiel, Tim Dunne

Dedication

This book is dedicated to my son Jett, whom I love more than life itself and my wife Kelly, who magically holds the key to Jett's first chapter and my second.

Acknowledgments

I would like to thank Linda Favila and her sister Christi for believing in my little book so much. And again Linda, for coordinating everything so well. Thank you, Susan Crawford—you believed that we could make a deal when no one else did; Jamie Raab, thank you for choosing this for Warner Books. I would like to acknowledge my best friend Anson Downes for helping me with the illustrations and Susan Such for organizing the original book. And finally, to the United ex-flight attendant Jean Anderson, who retyped my first manuscript and verified the authenticity of my detail . . . remember to fasten your seat belt and always keep your seat in an upright position.

Introduction

This book was conceived on a foggy night in the Fall of 1992 in a room at the Bangor Hilton Airport Hotel. My wife Kelly, my son Jett and I arrived at midnight, and the small plane that was to take us to the island where our Maine residence is was not cleared to go until the fog lifted in the early hours of the A.M.

Knowing I would not be able to sleep, I started to contemplate my love of aviation and reflect on my whole life, specifically in regard to some of my favorite memories and people related to air travel. I thought if perhaps I could create a fictitious situation mixed with some true personality types and stories I remembered over the years, I could create a fable that would be entertaining.

After seven hours of thought and a short flight to the island, all the elements of the story along with the sequence of events blended perfectly into new characters and scenarios. I was ready to type.

The first thing I did when I walked through the door was to pull out the typewriter, and for the

next ten days I would write. And each day after dinner, I would read to my wife Kelly, and my best friends Anson and Linda what I had written. After I was through writing, I started work on the illustrations and I asked Anson to do the finishing touches on the drawings. I printed up 75 copies exactly like the one being published now.

This book was originally meant only as a Christmas gift for my family, but it was passed along. And when about 200 readers responded to the book so positively, I decided to share it with everyone. Enjoy.

Thank you

John Travolta

I t was late at night and there was hardly anyone in the terminal. The voice over the P.A. system seemed so sophisticated, I imagined it belonged to someone really beautiful, more like an actress of some sort. "United Air Lines Flight 393 for Pittsburgh, Cleveland, and points west is now boarding at the West Arcade. All aboard please." The excitement ran through my body like nothing I had ever felt before. Knowing that within minutes I would be airborne for the first time was comparable to

nothing, including playing doctor with the kids on the block, and that was saying a lot for an eight-year-old.

I remember everything about that night — the lights being dim in the terminal; the colors of every airline insignia as we rushed to the gate in

the West Arcade. Even my mother seemed excited, but for totally different reasons, I'm sure. Probably something like the free drinks she could have, or the potential for meeting a handsome man on the plane. My mother was about forty-nine years old and quite attractive — blue eyes, black hair, and a good figure for her age, she told me.

2

She would have had an even better figure if she hadn't had me so late in life. And a lot of men didn't mind a little bit of a pot belly; it was very sexy to some, she thought. Maybe she would fall in love with someone really cool, like the captain of the plane or something, I thought.

Running through the Newark terminal was so much fun I couldn't believe we were actually going to fly this time. Most of our visits to the air-  port were to see people off. One time my mom actually had to fly to go to work in some play she was doing in summer stock. But this time I would get to go. It all seemed very surreal. My mom said, "Maybe if I act like Marilyn Monroe the ticket agent will put us in first class." She also said that all the drinks were on the house when you flew that way. Of course I didn't really care, as long as we got to really go.

That voice again, "Final call for United

Flight 393 for Pittsburgh, Cleveland, and points west, now boarding at gate 7. All aboard, please." Now my heart was in my throat. Everything around seemed as if it were in slow motion. As the ticket agent handed us our marked tickets, the door opened to the outside area where the aircraft sat awaiting our entrance. She was beautiful! Silver and white, with a blue stripe down the side with a red accent stripe and the letters "UNITED" printed on the side. Oh what a sight! The wind blew cold in my face, but it couldn't interrupt my first love affair. Noble in appearance, strong and powerful in impression, this would begin an experience I would never forget.

As we climbed the steps to board the aircraft I noticed something very peculiar. There weren't very many people boarding with us — only a few, really. Then I pretended that the flight was really only for me and my mother, and wasn't that unique! The stewardess at the top of the stairs was tall and slim and had a warm smile. She welcomed us and assured us that the inside of the cabin was warm.

There was something different about her. Something that was hard to pinpoint. Later my

mother would get to know her quite well. Almost best friends. I did ask her why Liz seemed so different from others, and my mom told me it was because she had depth and true sadness in her life from being in a concentration camp. After I knew that about Liz, I would have nightmares about being in a Nazi concentration camp myself. My mother let me sleep in the same bed with her until I was ten, or, as she told me, "Until I get a new husband." At any rate, any nightmare was not so bad because of it. But tonight I would join the evening stars.

As the engines started, one at a time, and I sat in what seemed a big, soft, comfortable chair, I could hardly hear them at all. The big propellers turned round as fire exited through the backside exhausts. I knew it was the "jet age," but there was something exciting about being in an aircraft that would take twice as long to get there as a jet would, especially my first time.

I had saved my coins in a floral-patterned ladies' purse that belonged to my mother. She told me that if I saved long enough we could go on a trip together. She would match my money.

Choosing a destination that would be inexpensive enough would be a somewhat pleasurable task. Little did I know that Mom was already planning a change-of-life move to Los Angeles.

There was nothing like it when my mother was excited about something. The whole world seemed to have brightness and hope. She told me the reason we were moving to Los Angeles was that a director friend of hers she worked with in Allentown had promised her that if she could get out west by February he could get her some work in film. Mom already had quite a few jobs as an "extra" under her belt, so it didn't seem that far-fetched. Also, she taught drama in school, and prior to that had a full-time stage career.

I had practically flown upstairs to the attic where I hid the airline schedules. United, TWA, American — these were the carriers that could take us there. United first, open to the back page where the air fares are listed. Then look for the most inexpensive fare possible. There it is, at the very end. PROPELLER ONE-WAY NIGHT COACH ($95) CHILDREN (half-fare). That's it, I thought. Now back to the flight times — night flight, night

6

flight; here we are. United Flight 393 departs at 9:00 P.M. DC-6 service to Los Angeles with intermittent stops at Pittsburgh, Cleveland, Chicago, Des Moines, Denver, Las Vegas, Los Angeles. Yes, that's it! Oh, yeah, it arrives at 3:00 P.M. the next day. What more could a kid ask for!

By the time I came back downstairs, the lights were off in the living room and the music from the radio portion of the stereo was playing softly: "Wives and Lovers," sung by Jack Jones. Her cigarette was burning in the dark, a glass of sherry by her side. Then I worried that what she had said about moving to Los Angeles might not be true — was it just a day dream of hers? Oh well, I thought, I could still just save for the short trip. Maybe I'll go up and count my change again.

We had a 1951 Ford station wagon that was kind of a muted green color. So there we were, in February, 1962, on our way to the Newark Airport with Flight 393 on my mind. She said when the odometer on the dash said "022" we'd be there. Now it was fun to see the big billboards that boasted of different flying opportunities one could take, like "Fly Eastern to

Miami non-stop,'' etc. And here I am on this plane, going on the farthest trip the airline offers. Wow!

There were a total of about fifteen people on this first segment of the flight. I was wearing a hunter's cap that I forgot to remove, probably due to coming in from the cold. Nevertheless, on take-off this was my look. I could tell that my mother was excited for me, but for the moment was kind of impatiently waiting to be airborne, so she could have a cigarette and a drink. As we sped down the runway that surreal

8

feeling came over me again. "I can't believe I'm flying," I told her. She smiled at me, and at that moment the aircraft left the ground. I'll always remember my mother that way. The take-off was much more gentle in feeling than I thought it would be. For some reason everything that happened thus far that night seemed perfect. For years after, no matter what negative experience I might have, from the time I would leave for the airport until the time I would arrive at my destination, life would seem safe and I would be happy.

My mother liked Manhattans. Just before we leveled off at our altitude, Liz showed up by the side of our seats and asked what we would like to drink. I immediately asked for a Coke and Mom asked for a Manhattan along with confirmation that she could smoke. Newport filter cigarettes. That turquoise box, that half-moon in the middle of it, would always bring to mind pleasurable memories. As she lights up and that first satisfying breath of smoke leaves her mouth, I would think "how festive." Smoke meant show business and good times. All of Mom's friends from the theater smoked. As a matter of fact, I don't

remember an adult who didn't.

I could see every star in the night, or so it seemed as I looked out the window. This is so beautiful. "Why don't people just live in airplanes?" I started to reflect on how sometimes at home, late at night, I would lie in bed awake, listening to the drone of some airplane flying over my house, probably just having left Newark or La Guardia airport. And I would think "Where is that plane going this late at night? And who's on it, anyway? Are they sleeping? Are there beds on board?" And here I am, maybe even on that very same plane I had been pondering.

When I turned my head from the window, Liz had returned from the galley with our drinks, explaining that the gentleman in seat 4E had treated her to the cocktail. "Oh," my mother said. "How nice. Please tell him thank you." When my mother wanted to impress someone, often her voice got deeper and richer. I called it her "theatrical voice." She didn't like it when I would say it, but it never stopped her from using it. Shortly after, almost like clockwork, a most handsome gentleman, about fifty-five, sat across from us in the same aisle. My mother at once

wondered if this indeed was the gentleman who had treated her to the drink. She suddenly started to act nervous out of nowhere. Puzzling, I thought. Then the gentleman said, "Do you mind if I sit next to you?" "If you don't, I'll pull you over," my mother replied. I thought, "What's that comment all about?" My mother proceeded to tell him how nervous she was about flying. "You are not," I said. "Don't get smart with me," she said. "But you're not," I insisted. By this time I had totally ruined her come-on. "Why don't you go up to the cockpit and see if you could meet the pilots," she said. Actually that was a good idea, even though I thought I was probably in trouble. So I left my mother to her own devices and proceeded up the aisle.

I was half way to the cockpit when I saw what seemed to be the most bizarre sight: This extraordinarily tall man was blocking my way. I looked up and he said, "Hello, I'm the ten-foot-tall man. Would you like my autograph?" "Who are you?" I asked. "I work for Barnum & Bailey's circus. I'm the ten-foot-tall man." "Okay," I said, to totally appease him. He gave me a photo, pre-signed, and I proceeded to go to the cockpit.

Again this kind of surrealistic incident.

In the early sixties the cockpit doors were not locked, and one could have easy access to them, usually with permission from the stewardess. Liz was not to be found, so I opened the door to the cockpit anyway. There were three men, facing forward, so they didn't see me enter. I only caught part of the story one was telling. But it was about some stewardess they had all flown with and how she treated the crew really well and that at the end of some trip to Boston from Washington they were all quite satisfied. Only later did I realize, when I was older, that they were probably referring to sex or something.

At any rate, their faces seemed flushed even in the dark when they realized I was in the cockpit, without knowing how long I had been there. "Well, hello," said the man whose story I had interrupted. "Going to Pittsburgh tonight?" "No," I said with pride, "Los Angeles." A small burst of laughter came from at least two of them. "How did you ever end up on the milk run?" the captain asked. Suddenly I went flush. A million thoughts went through my head. But then the truth came blaring out. "I wanted to stay on the

plane as long as I possibly could and my mother can't afford a non-stop jet." There. I said it, almost in tears. I thought they would have loved the idea that I liked planes so much, but they saw the more inconvenient side of it, I guess.

"Well, we're only with you until Chicago, but when and if you get bored, you're welcome to come up and visit. But ask the stewardess first, okay?" "Sure," I said. I left the cockpit kind of miffed a bit. Nevertheless I was flying, and all night at that. Could life be better?

By the time I got back to my seat, Mom was on her second drink and already getting very touchy with her new friend Harry. "This is my baby boy Jeff and this is Harry. Harry lives in Pittsburgh, honey. He's a lawyer and knows some of the Pittsburgh Steelers. Isn't that wild?" I nodded my head "Yes" and proceeded to ask him if he was married and had any children. My mother gave me the look that meant I was being rude. Then he confidently said, "Why, yes, I am, and I have a boy and a girl." "Oh," I said. "That's good." Then I left to go to the back of the plane toward the galley area where Liz was preparing some sort of hot food. "I hope you like chicken," she said. "I

like *fried* chicken." "Well, this is just like it. It's called chicken cordon bleu, and it's very tasty." "Okay, I'll have some," I said.

When I got back to my seat Harry was whispering something in my mother's ear. I waited until I thought he was through so I wouldn't get in trouble. He got up and left his seat and I got back in mine. "Oh, what a wonderful man," she said. "So well spoken." My mother liked people who spoke well and enunciated words and were articulate. She didn't like accents too much on people unless they were using them for a role. She said good speech reflected how well educated they were. Her friend Julia was a beautiful woman, very wealthy, married to a rich inventor, and seemed to have it all, except my mother could never get over the idea that she had a thick New Jersey accent. She would say "What a shame. All that beauty and wealth and that horrible New Jersey accent." The funny thing was that sometimes Mom would actually have an accent herself. "If we were ever in Pittsburgh one day, Harry would love to take us out to dinner." "Oh. With his wife and kids," I said. "Smart ass," she scolded.

As the darkness of the night turned into

snow clouds outside the window, I could sense something being placed before me, and from the smell of it, it was chicken cordon bleu. Wow! It really did look like fried chicken, but better. "Could I have another Coke?" I started to dig  in and cheese dripped out from the center of the chicken. Oh, I like chicken, and I like cheese, but I'm not sure I can eat them together. So I picked at it for a while and thought, "Maybe when we get to Pittsburgh, Mom will buy me a grilled cheese or a hot dog. Until then, perhaps I'll eat this dessert and drink as many Cokes as possible."

As we started our descent into the Pittsburgh area, I could finally see out the window. We were below the cloud layer now, and it was snowing at a pretty good rate. It actually looked quite beautiful to see the city below kind of glisten through the weather. Then I started to think that possibly there was some child down below in some

house, listening to the drone of the engines above and wondering who was on that plane so late and where they were going and were they sleeping or not.

We could hardly feel the landing, it was so smooth. The blue lights that lined the taxiway seemed to stand out even more in the snowstorm. As we taxied up to the gate, an announcement over the P.A. system on the plane was being made. "This is your captain speaking. Due to the unexpected snowstorm, those of you continuing on to Cleveland and Chicago will be delayed until further notice. Please check with the ticket agent at the gate for further information." Wow, I thought, pretty interesting. Liz stopped by our seats before we got up to leave and told us not to worry, that United would be taking care of a hotel for the passengers free of charge. The hotel simply stated "Airport Hotel" and had a neon light in the shape of a four-engine propeller airliner. I loved dates and trivia, so I asked the man behind the counter when the hotel was built. "In 1951, I believe," he said. "Oh thank you," I responded. Now I could

fantasize about all the people who had to do the same thing we were doing in the middle of the night for the last eleven years. Wow!

My mother told me that the airline would call the room when the flight was ready, but it wouldn't be for at least a couple of hours, so I should get some sleep. She was going to get a nightcap in the lounge downstairs. Somehow I knew Harry was going to be involved, but I held my tongue.

Ring, ring. What's that? I thought. Oh, the phone. Right. The airline must be calling, it's 3:00 A.M. I better pick it up. "Hello. Yes, we'll be there." I ran out the door, flew down the hallway and pushed all the elevator buttons. What a jerk. Why did you do that? As I looked down the hall, I saw Mom leave some different room. It didn't really matter, even if she was with Harry. What really mattered was that we had only about twenty minutes to get to the gate to continue our flight.

For three in the morning my mother was in an awfully good mood. But so was I. Three hours of sleep and the rest of our journey to go.

The flight from Pittsburgh to Cleveland was just under an hour long, and was far more interesting in retrospect because from a distance I watched my mother sit with Liz. The airplane was virtually empty, so Liz gave me a Coke and I sat across the aisle from them, looked out the window, and watched my mother go through more emotions in forty minutes than I had ever seen before. Crying, laughing, looking frightened, then mad. I thought, what could she be telling her? Later, of course, I got the whole story on Liz. She had actually come from a very wealthy Jewish family in Germany. She was only twelve when they had tried to flee the country. She and her older brother were the only ones to make it, and unfortunately had to watch her family die. There was a TV show in the New York area at the time called "Remember Us." It showed actual footage of the Nazi event that was probably more responsible for my nightmares than anything. I just always felt bad for Liz. Anyway, my mother really cared for Liz. It was almost as if someone in more emotional pain than her offered some kind of relief.

I suddenly was sorry I hadn't gotten to

know the ten-foot-tall man. At least it would have been someone to talk to.

We decided to stay on board during the stop in Cleveland. Mom and I actually got a nap in. We were in the air again before we awakened. Liz let us sleep as long as we were buckled up. No one had gotten on in Cleveland who seemed that interesting. At four in the morning why would they? So we slept until Chicago. It was still dark when we arrived in the somewhat new O'Hare terminal. When I asked what time it was Liz said 4:00 A.M. I asked how that could be. I learned about the time change to Central Standard Time.

The terminal was beautiful, and for some reason the hot dog stand was open even at four in the morning. I wanted two, and Mom said in her decidedly theatrical voice, "Do you reeeally reeeally want another hot dog?" I was suddenly taken aback. There was no one there to impress but me. So I said, "Yes, I reeeally do." How could life be any better? An empty airport, four in the morning, and two hot dogs and a Coke.

Unbelievable as it might seem, life did get better. When we returned to the gate, to board the Des Moines part of the trip, Liz was waiting

for us. She told us that this was where she got off. Chicago was her base, and a new crew would be taking over for the rest of the trip. I felt a loss having to say good-by to Liz. She told my mother that she had arranged a surprise for me in Denver. But the news that overwhelmed both my mother and me was that Liz had fixed it so we would fly the rest of the trip first class! My mother was visibly moved by the thoughtfulness of this gesture. All I could think about was how much it would have cost us if we had to pay for it ourselves. It was something like $185 one way, the amount of toys and hot dogs I could buy, and that's including probably two to three more trips like this. What a gal, that Liz.

Suddenly my mother's whole demeanor changed. I could see the visible change come over her. Her posture was straight, her chin up, and her walk noble. We were flying "first class." And she was an actress flying to the West Coast "first class." She quickly told the ticket agent her reasons. "Hollywood called. They told me to grab the next flight." The ticket agent, mildly interested, said, "Oh, are you an actress?" "Why, yes," my mother responded. "How did you guess?" When my

mother was a little too contented or really excited about something, she often would make unsolicited comments like this. I just know she was wishing she had worn the fake leopard coat I had talked her out of before we left the house. This was before the days when fake furs were in vogue. I would tell her things like, "Oh, you think you're rich," or "Walk ahead of me so my friends don't see me with you in that coat." But this time I really wished she could have walked on board with her first class ticket and her leopard coat.

The first class sections on propeller planes were usually in the back of the plane, different from the jets. The first thing I noticed was that the seats were bigger, only two to a side of each aisle. When we took off it was much more quiet. That's probably the reason the seating was placed in the back. In jets, it's quieter up front. I see. My mother seemed genuinely excited to be flying in first class. She told me that if she were being flown out by a film studio, the Screen Actors Guild would demand the studio fly you this way. "It's the rules," she said. As the plane continued to fly westward, I could see the sun was starting to rise. As we did a small turn to the right, the sun came through the

window and seemed as if it were dancing on my mother's face. She was starting to doze off, and I thought she really was meant to have the good things in life, she appreciates them so much. She really should have been Barbara Stanwyck or Kate Hepburn. She was as good as they were. She told me so. One review in stock said of her performance in *Light Up the Sky,* "She is a cross between Crawford and Stanwyck, a tour-de-force performance." We have the actual clipping.

I looked up toward the right side portion of the ceiling. There was a kind of buckle and strap apparatus, and I couldn't quite figure out its purpose. I looked up and down the aisle for that really pretty stewardess, Doris. She finally appeared from inside the galley. I motioned to her just the way I would have to my teacher at school. "Yes," she said, "may I help you?" Her voice seemed so familiar. When she welcomed us aboard over the aircraft's P.A. system, she sounded just like the voice I heard at the Newark Airport terminal. And she looked exactly how I imagined that person would look. "What's that for?" I asked. "Oh, that's the berthing for the cross-country overnight flights. We don't really use them anymore." My interest now peaked.

"When did you use them? What year? How come you stopped? How many are there?" "Well," she said, "I'll answer one question at a time." "Okay," I said. "Well, from about 1947 when this plane was new until the jets came in, in 1959. This was used on longer non-stop flights, any time the plane flew, let's say, over seven hours. Let's say on an overnight flight cross country, we would sleep people. That was part of the first class airfare." "Oh, cool," I responded. "How come you know so much?" "Well," she proceeded, "my grandmother has been in the airline industry for years, originally as a stewardess in the thirties." "Wow," I said. "She retired in 1939 and ever since then has been doing the flight announcements at Newark Airport." On that note she started to leave, and I flew down the aisle after her. "You're kidding. Really? How old is she now? What kind of planes did she fly in? Where does she say those announcements from in the airport?" Doris answered all my questions and more. She was my new best friend.

"Mom. Mom, wake up. You gotta wake up." "What is it?" she said. "You're not going to believe this. Doris's grandma is the voice at Newark Airport. She's seventy-two years old, and she was

one of the first stewardesses ever. Mom, you're gonna love her — she has no accent at all and she's really beautiful!'' "Who?" asked my mother. "Doris!!!!" "That's wonderful, my baby boy." "Don't call me that in front of Doris, okay?" "Okay," she said. "Now let me go back to sleep."

Doris was preparing the beverage order for the passengers. Her blond hair was done in just the style I liked, teased on top, a French twist in

 the back. Blue eyes. I couldn't stop looking at her. "How old are you?" "Twenty-one," she said with a smile. "What's your favorite airplane?" "The Caravelle," she answered. "Why?" I asked. "It's beautiful to look at and it's all first class. Easier to serve the customers." "That's pretty good," I said. "Do you have a boyfriend?" "I did, but we just broke up." "My mother's an actress, you know." I used this line whenever I wanted to impress someone. "Really. That's very interesting." "Yes, we're going

to Hollywood. They called her. She has to do some movie with Paul Newman, I think." "Paul Newman," she said. "Paul Newman. I can't believe it." "Well, I gotta go. My mother wanted something." "Okay," she said. Oh God, why did I lie? That was so stupid. She was already impressed with just the actress stuff.

The Des Moines Airport was not very interesting, really. However, the gift store was open and I couldn't wait to see if there were any cool toys there. Oh, my God, oh, my God, there's a battery-powered toy replica of the same airplane we're on. Each engine starts, one at a time, it lights up, the door opens, the passengers disappear, and the door closes again. Then it starts to taxi. It was the greatest toy ever made, bar none. Oh, please Mom, please please could I have it? I'll do anything you ask. Please.

Life at this moment was so good that — well, it was just hard to recover from. Until I stepped on the tail of my new plane. I didn't stop crying for about an hour, including the time during take-off en route to Denver. This would be our longest leg, just under four hours, due to head

winds. Finally Doris made some sense. "Even real planes break," she said. As if the Lord himself had spoken, I stopped crying and said, "They do?" "Yes, of course they do," she added. "Oh." It made so much sense that I perked up immediately and said, "Well, I'll just get it fixed, then." Doris's telling me that changed my life forever. I had always had a problem with things being less than perfect for some reason, especially mechanical things. And now she had the answer I would use until this day. Real things break too. She felt so bad about my toy breaking that she offered to make up the berth so I could get some sleep. My mother said it

wouldn't be necessary. But I had to beg to differ at this time. I was so excited to be in this berth looking out into the sky from the little window

above that I couldn't sleep at all. But I wanted to stay put so I could have some fun, maybe even eat my meal up here.

At that point I overheard Doris congratulating my mother on the Paul Newman film. I could hear my mother laugh and bail me out at the same time. "He must have misunderstood. There is no specific film. Just a friend who was going to try and help out. He knows I like Paul Newman as an actor and somehow put the two together." I was mortified and didn't want to live anymore. I buried my face in the pillow and waited for lunch to be served.

I could smell lunch coming. "I hope you like chicken," Doris said. "I like *fried* chicken," I replied. "Well, this is just like it only better." "Oh yeah," I said. "It's chicken cordon bleu." My face dropped and I asked for another Coke.

From where I was sitting, which was on the upper berth, I could almost see everyone forward of me, mainly the coach passengers. I watched them closely, between referring to the description of my new toy plane on the side of the box it had come in and admiring the colorful sketchlike image of the plane on the top of the

box. I couldn't quite confront the broken plane inside. I would wait until after it was fixed.

The man in the seat I approximated to be 7D was drinking a lot and smoking Pall Malls, a very strong unfiltered cigarette, my mother once told me. Newports were not nearly as strong. At any rate, he kept referring to the headline on the front of what appeared to be the *Des Moines Daily News*. It said, "DISASTER: JET AIRLINER CRASHES AT IDLEWILD," and below was some blurry black-and-white photo. Air crashes when I was younger were more intriguing to me than upsetting. I think it was just too much to comprehend that something I loved so much could ever hurt anyone, let alone kill them. He started to shake and perspire as I watched him fumble through the paper. Then I saw a different stewardess, not Doris, start to talk to him. I had no idea what she said, but he did seem to calm down a bit. I found out later, through Doris, that that same gentleman, two years ago, had actually booked himself on an evening flight from Chicago to New York and when he arrived at the airport found the airline had sold his spot to someone else. He fought and fought with the ticket agent, but to no avail. He

left the airport already deciding that the next day would be better anyway. On the news that night, they reported that the very same plane he had fought so hard to get on had crashed in the bay at La Guardia Airport on final approach, due to weather.

I guess he had a right to be scared. Besides, how could I make him feel any better; my plane had a broken tail. It would probably scare him just to look at it.

I just had the greatest idea! Maybe the captain could fix it. My toy, that is. As the captain removed a small pliers out of his flight bag, I asked him if he was married. "No, I'm not. Freshly divorced." "Isn't that a coincidence, my mother's an actress." I don't think I knew what a coincidence was. He fixed it. God, he's the greatest. Why couldn't he marry my mother. "Thank you," I said.

Then one last desperate move. "You know, my mother is going to be in a movie with I think she said Kirk Douglas and Marilyn Monroe." No response. I waited another beat. "And Paul Newman." "Really? Paul Newman?" "Yes," I said. "I have to go now. Thank you."

A s I approached the first class section I could see that my mother was now awake, and my berth hadn't been put up yet. "Hello, darling," she said. She looked really pleased and I knew why. Fresh linen had just been placed before her and the most beautiful china and silverware for her to look at. "Lenox," she said, as she peered down the aisle to make sure no one was looking. Then she turned the plate to show me. Mom loved antiques and expensive china. She told me that it was ill-mannered to turn a plate over in front of people when it was set before you. She started to read aloud the menu, a habit that she had. It was done in a very deep theatrical voice that always embarrassed me at restaurants. "Your choice of appetizer, shrimp cocktail or stuffed mushroom with crab meat. Main course, beef with au jus or . . ." I chimed in, "CHICKEN CORDON BLEU." I jumped out of my seat, already bored with my mother for now. I climbed back up to my little haven, my own private world. As I looked down at where my mother was sitting, I wondered what we would do this year for my birthday. I started to giggle at the thought of when I was little, my fifth birthday. It was so successful

that I wanted a party every day. My mother gave in for about five days. I then had to learn the ugly truth. Birthdays lasted only one day, usually.

But no one told me that I couldn't have them every month. I can remember that one time in April my mother's friend walked in on one of my birthdays and said, "Isn't his birthday in February?" "Yes," my mother said, "but don't spoil it for him." My mom was good that way. I turned over on to my back. The drone of the engines seemed to be kind of lulling me. Before I knew it I was asleep. For many years to come I would scrounge through my airline schedules to find a propeller plane to fly, providing I had the time, just so I could get that same kind of sleep.

I was awakened by the sound of a *ding,* and the pressure of someone's hand. It was Doris. "You can stay up here as long as you stay strapped in." "Okay," I said. "This is your captain speaking. We're expecting moderate turbulence for about the next twenty minutes. Please remain seated and fasten your seat belts."

The aircraft started to buffet and rumble a bit. The pitch of the engines' sound changed as we started to climb above the weather. However

the turbulence got worse and some of the passengers started to look around as if maybe something they could look at would solve this problem. The man in 12A ran back to the lounge area in the very back of the plane. The stewardess that I didn't know ran after him. When they had both arrived at the lounge area, she closed the curtain. Now I was curious as ever to find out what was going on. I squirmed my way to the

back of my berth and peeked through the curtain. What a bizarre sight! The man had his hands around the throat of the young lady and she had her hands around his throat as well. There seemed to be genuine resistance between the two. But they were having a quite normal conversation. There was more to this character than meets the eye. When he boarded before everyone else, apparently he was drugged and placed on board so he could be transferred to a different mental

hospital in Denver. Apparently he came to, and realized his situation and wanted to get off the plane. They were talking in such a calm manner it was hard to believe anything was wrong.

I tried to flag down Doris. She finally caught my look and came over. I explained what was happening, and she quickly went to assist. The other stewardess told her that she was fine and could Doris just take over her duties for a while. Doris knew better and got the first officer, and together they managed to calm him down. Still, everyone was quite uneasy until we disembarked. As we were exiting the plane, the captain saw me coming down the aisle. He then looked up at my mother, gave a most radiant smile, and said, "Good luck on that Paul Newman film." My mom looked at me disapprovingly and very politely looked at the captain and said, "Why thank you, I'll need it."

We went to lunch at the Denver terminal. Grilled cheese and a Coke, as I watched the airplanes come and go. This was just great. What could happen to beat everything that happened so far? Nothing. I want-

ed to live forever. By this time I had forgotten about my surprise that Liz had arranged at the Denver Airport. When we arrived at the gate, I with my rather large souvenir lollipop with "Denver" written in the middle and my dearly beloved toy airplane in a box, I said to my mother in a truly insistent manner, "We're at the wrong gate, Mom! We're gonna miss the plane! It's not this one, Mom, I'm telling you, it's not!" She ignored me and proceeded to give our tickets to the agent. "We're gonna be so embarrassed. This is a non-stop jet flight to L.A. I know it by heart. The 5:00 P.M. Caravelle service executive flight, men only." Only a few cities offered this. Denver was one. We couldn't be on it even if we wanted to.

"Yes," the flight agent said. "Liz told me all about it." My mother nodded with a knowing smile. Suddenly life went unreal again. It couldn't be, we're not, really? I could hardly open my mouth. Then Mom said, "Surprise, honey. We're going on a jet to L.A." "I can't believe it." I went too silent. Mother wondered what was wrong. She said, "Aren't you excited, Baby? This is your surprise from Liz." I was truly. I just didn't know how to express it sometimes, that's all.

I did feel a loss of some sort, a combination of saying good-by to that big old beautiful plane and never seeing Doris again. I started to cry. Mom asked, "What's wrong, honey?" I just couldn't explain it all to her, so something really stupid came out of my mouth like, "*You,* the only woman on an all men's flight!" She didn't say anything and I felt really bad as we climbed the ramp to this absolutely perfect specimen of an aircraft. It was art, believe me. The French built the Caravelle, the same company that later went on to help design the Concorde.

Now it all seemed to make sense. Yesterday when we got off in Denver, Mom made up a story about our plane having a mechanical breakdown, and that we would have to stay overnight in Denver. The truth must have been that Liz told her that if we could manage to stay in Denver overnight, she could arrange the jet flight. In other words, if we had the time, United had the money. Actually, staying in Denver was fun. That night Mom read me two acts of a play. Ever since I can remember, Mom read me good-night plays instead of fairy tales.

I think last night's play was *Philadelphia Story*.

I remember the Caravelle jet had unusual-looking windows, triangular in shape. It was an all one-class aircraft, the way United had it, all first class. There were about twenty on board that evening, less than half-full. My mother sat in the back of the jet, near the crew. She was flying as a United employee. That's how Liz was able to get us on and allow Mother on an all men's flight. I, how-

ever, got to sit wherever I liked. I sat in the very front row, all by myself, on purpose, so I could imagine what it would be like to do so. Strapped

in, ready for take-off, the aircraft turned to depart the active runway. A surge of power thrust me back in the seat. I felt as though I was pinned. Already quite different from the docile feeling of the DC-6. Then straight up in the air. "Wow," I said to myself. This is fantastic, I thought. And it was. We were over the Colorado mountains before we knew it. The snowcapped mountains at sunset were unforgettable. As we leveled off in what seemed just minutes, I decided to roam the cabin. Maybe just for a minute I would break my pretense of being alone and visit Mother. On the way to my mother's seat, I was walking in a very cocky manner, a way that only an eight-year-old could do when he knows he is doing something truly special. As I looked to the left, midway down the aisle, I saw a young kid there, older than me, about ten maybe. His face was buried in an airline schedule. It said "United, effective March, 1962." "Is that the new one?" I asked him. The face of a redheaded braced-faced boy looked up at me, stared right into my eyes and said, "My dad gets them in the mail before anyone else does." I said, "God, you're so lucky." "That was the beginning of a beautiful friendship," to quote Humphrey Bogart in

Casablanca. "I'll be right back," I said. I ran back to tell my mother.

She was sitting with a woman I figured was also an employee of United, about Mom's age, very pretty, and just how my mother liked, sophisticated, wealthy, and no accent. Her story was that her father actually owned an airline. "Trans-Caribbean Airlines." Her name was put on the front of the nose of one of the newly acquired DC-8 jets. Also she was quite sad due to the fact that her husband had just passed away. He was on the podium, accepting his presidency of the Crocker Bank of California, when he suffered a heart attack. What a dilemma. Do I stay and bend her ear about the airlines or do I contribute to my beautiful new friendship? Mom's crying; I think I'll go talk to Skipper — that was his name.

The next hour was filled with conversation that would only fascinate Skipper and myself, that is, can you believe that TWA had a nonstop

Constellation flight from San Francisco to London up to 1960? It took twenty-two hours! Wow! Really, etc. To think that just last night I had self-pity, thinking if only my friends could see me now . . . They wouldn't care, they don't like aviation. And now I have Skipper. "Where is your father?" I asked. "Over there," he said. Across the aisle was a man who looked like a movie star. "What does he do?" "Oh, he's a lawyer," Skip said. "Where's your mom?" "Oh, she died when I was three." "Oh, really. Do you have a new mother?" I asked. "No, my dad remarried twice after Mom died and they died, too, cancer, all of them." "You're kidding," I said. "Does your dad have an accent?" "What?" he responded. "Does he have an accent?" "I don't know," he said. "Does it matter?" "Well, yeah, kind of." "I don't think he does." "Oh, great," I said, "my mom's gonna love him. She loves people without accents."

"Mom, you're not gonna believe, I found a new best friend and his dad is rich, sad, and doesn't have an accent." Both ladies laughed at my expense. I was interrupted by a "Hi." I looked up as if I was dreaming. Doris was there. My face flushed as she bent down to kiss me. I'll never

wash my face again. This is too good, my girlfriend, my buddy, my mom's new husband (hopefully), and we're all on a new jet heading westward. It's scientifically impossible for life to be any better.

But I was wrong. The dark-haired stewardess was serving us up front. "Do you like chicken?" Oh, no, I thought. I said apathetically, "Not really." Then she said, "You don't like fried chicken?" "I love fried chicken," I said, with a sudden hope. "Well," she continued, "it's just like it. It's called chicken cordon bleu." I crumpled. She noticed my disappointment as she said, "But on our jet flights we offer a children's menu, which is your choice of hot dog, cheeseburger, or peanut butter and jelly sandwich." I thought I would faint, a hot dog at 30,000 feet, I can't believe it. I was so excited I was lost for words, but I had to say something so I turned to Skip and said, "I like your braces." The comment kind of stayed stupidly in the air. But just minutes later it didn't matter. The sun was set, the stars were out, and I was eating a hot dog and drinking a Coke with my new best friend at 500 m.p.h. From that moment on I never thought things couldn't get better than they were.

As we taxied in, I could see the new

space-age–style restaurant at LAX. It was truly beautiful. I would really like to eat there sometime, I thought. Through the window I could see the jetway start to glide over to meet our plane. There was some commotion at the large opening of the portable gate. Cameras and motion picture lights were there, seeming to prepare for something. It was the captain of our jet. He was sixty-two years old and this was his last flight, and *Life* magazine was doing a TV special on him. It was all so exciting, arriving in Hollywood and all this happening. Mom caught wind of this and a panic came over her. She started to check out her makeup. Mom put her lipstick on with a brush, a small one. It was so interesting to watch her apply it. She acted as though she were painting her lips on canvas, an important piece of work. I overheard the interviewer ask the captain a question, "What are you going to do with your wings, now that you're retired?" "Well, I'm not officially retired until I sign out," he said. "However, if I'm forced to retire before your cameras, I guess I'll have to give my wings to the young man here who seems to have flying in his blood." I thought he meant Skipper, but at that moment he bent down and pinned the wings on me.

Epilogue

I took that moment in my life so seriously that today I'm a captain for United Airlines. I married Doris, although I had some catching up to do, seventeen years, to be exact. But nevertheless happily married, an aviation couple to the max. As a matter of fact, I get to see her almost every day. She's the new voice at Newark Airport, and I've got the New York–L.A. run. Very convenient. Oh, yeah, in case you were wondering about Mom, she never married Skipper's dad, but she did get to date him for a while. We all pretended that it would work out. She's very happy, though. She teaches acting at the Pasadena Playhouse in California. She's eighty now, and gets a big kick out of the young guys. And Liz is her favorite student, has been for almost twenty years.

It's been a wonderful life.

The End